First published in the United States, Great Britain, Canada, Australia, and New Zealand
in 2008 by North-South Books Inc., an imprint of NordSüd Verlag AG, Zürich, Switzerland.
Distributed in the United States by North-South Books Inc., New York.

Library of Congress Cataloging-in-Publication Data is available.
ISBN: 978-0-7358-2209-2 (trade edition).
2 4 6 8 10   9 7 5 3 1
Printed in Belgium.

www.northsouth.com

FSC
Mixed Sources
Product group from well-managed
forests and other controlled sources
Cert no. BV-COC-070303
www.fsc.org
© 1996 Forest Stewardship Council

Little Polar Bear
and the *Whales*

Hans de Beer

NorthSouth
New York / London

Lars, the little polar bear, lived at the North Pole in the middle of snow and ice. So far north, the winter is long and dark. But today, it was spring at last. "How nice and warm!" thought Lars.

Not everyone was happy about the warm weather. "It's too warm," Lars's father grumbled. But Lars liked it. The melting snow made some fine pools, and he enjoyed a morning bath in one of them.

After his bath, Lars took a walk in the spring sunshine. He sniffed the fresh air. Small plants and flowers were sprouting here and there through the melting snow.

But what was this? There was something strange poking out of the ice. There were ropes and masts and sails. It was a shipwreck! Lars scrambled down to investigate.

"Who's there?" squawked a voice. Lars jumped. A strange bird was perched on the edge of a rowboat, spreading his wings.

"Looks like you've never seen a cormorant before," said the bird.

"Uh, no sir, I haven't," said Lars politely.

The bird chuckled. "That's because I'm not usually around here," he said. "But it's been so warm, I just kept coming north. My name's Conrad, by the way. Conny for short."

"I'm Lars," said Lars. "What are you going to do here?"

"Go fishing, of course," said Conny. "I'm going to fish with the white whales."

"You mean the belugas?" said Lars, amazed.

"Yes," said Conny. "Why don't you come with me to the big bay and meet them. You run on ahead. It's too hard for me to walk in this slush. I'll fly instead. Meet you there!"

While they waited for the belugas at the big bay, Conny explained about the shipwreck.

"That was an old whaling boat," said Conny. "In the olden days, they sailed all around the world, killing whales."

"How awful!" said Lars.

Suddenly Lars heard a loud splash. The belugas!

"Don't be frightened," said Conny. "They're all very nice."

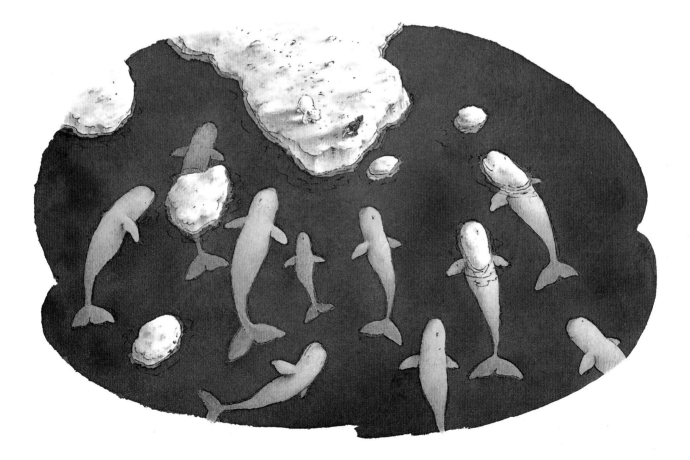

Before long, Lars was diving and playing right in the middle of the belugas. He made friends with a young whale named Bella.

All at once Conny leaped onto a chunk of ice. *"LOOK OUT!"* he squawked. "Quick! Get away! You're in danger!"

A huge gray whale suddenly rose up beside them. He looked as big as a mountain. "The bird is right," he said in a deep, rumbling voice.

"Who are you?" Lars asked.

"I'm Moby," said the giant sperm whale. "A whaling ship is after me. It's been following me for days. We're all in danger."

"What are we going to do?" cried Bella.

"I have an idea," Lars shouted. "There's a little bay behind those glaciers. The entrance is too narrow for a ship, but you'll be able to get in. You can hide there until the ship goes away."

The whales raced for the small bay. The entrance was narrow, but Moby managed to squeeze in too.

The whales hid under the water as the whaling ship drew closer. Lars and Conny hid behind some rocks.

"They're not supposed to kill whales anymore," said Conny angrily.

At sunset, the ship turned on its searchlights, but the whales' heads just looked like more rocks and ice floes.

The next morning, the ship was far away on the horizon. The whales resurfaced. They were safe!

"Hooray for Lars!" they cheered.

But soon there was more trouble. In the warm spring air, the ice had been melting. Now part of the glacier was falling off! Large chunks of ice crashed into the water.

The way out of the bay was blocked. The whales were trapped!
"How will we ever get out of here again?" Moby groaned.
"How indeed?" said Conny.

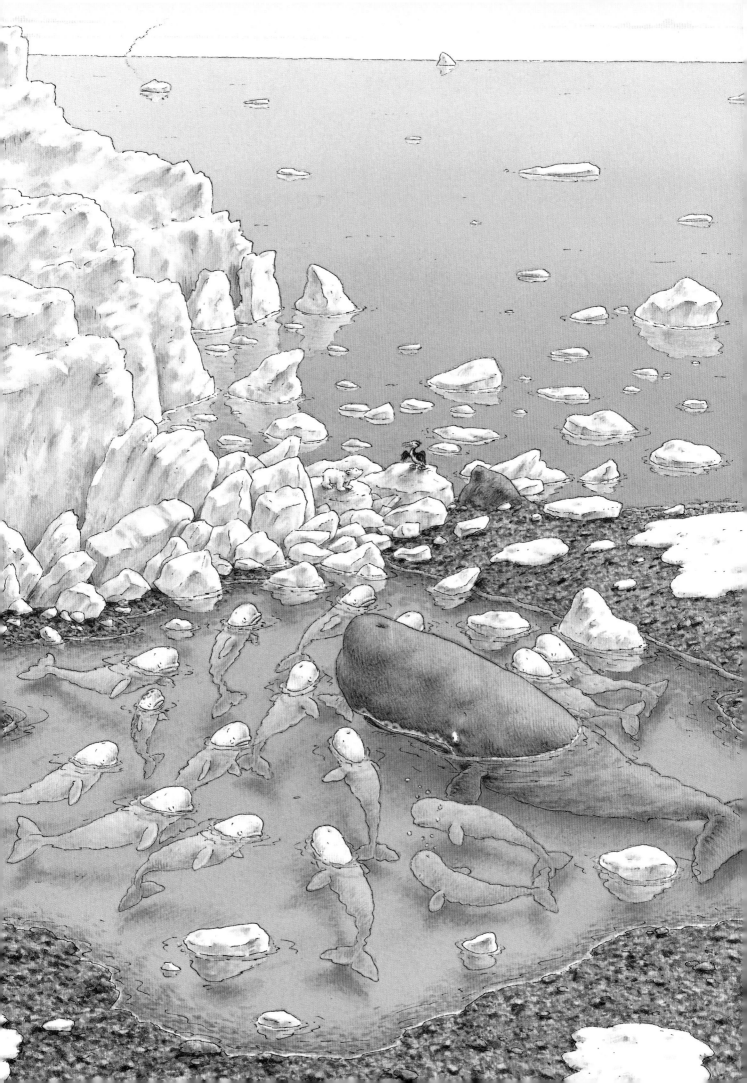

"Conny, I've got it!" Lars shouted. "The shipwreck's sails! That's the solution! But we'll need my mother and father to help."

While Conny flew off to get Lars's mother and father, Lars started untying a huge sail. When they came, he told his parents what he had in mind.

Lars's father was very proud. "What a smart young bear we have," he said. "Just like his father."

Then the polar bears dragged the heavy sail to the bay.

They stretched the sail across the ice dam. Lars wet it to make it slippery.

"You can slide right over to the other side now!" he told the whales. "Swim fast!"

The first belugas took a run up and—*WHOOSH!*—over the sail they went, into the open sea.

But Bella was frightened. "I'm too little," she cried.

"You can make it," Lars encouraged her. "The sail is nice and smooth."

Soon Bella and her mother were over the sail and into the sea.

Finally only Moby was left in the bay.

"Here I come!" he rumbled. And with an enormous leap and a gigantic *SPLASH!* the giant sperm whale was over the top.

What a celebration there was then! Moby tossed Lars up in the air while the happy belugas swam around them.

"Would you just look at that!" said Conny to Lars's mother and father.

And then it was time to say good-bye.

"Come back and play again!" Lars called to Bella.

"We will!" Bella promised

On the way home it began to snow.

"What a pity," said Conny. "It was so nice and warm."

But Lars's father was happy. "We like the cold," he said.

And Lars, the little polar bear, agreed.